The Witch's Children and the Queen

ORCHARD BOOKS

96 Leonard Street, London EC2A 4XD

Orchard Books Australia

Unit 32/45-51 Huntley Street, Alexandria, NSW 2015

First published in Great Britain in 2003

First paperback publication in 2004

ISBN 1 84121 416 7 (hardback)

ISBN 1 84362 036 7 (paperback)

Text © Ursula Jones 2003

Illustrations © Russell Ayto 2003

The rights of Ursula Jones to be identified as the author and

of Russell Ayto to be identified as the illustrator of this work

have been asserted by them in accordance with the

Copyright, Designs and Patents Act, 1988.

A CIP catalogue record for this book is available

from the British Library.

(hardback) 10 9 8 7 6 5 4 3 2 1

(paperback) 10 9 8 7 6 5 4 3

Printed in Belgium

The Witch's Children and the Queen

Written by

Ursula Jones

Illustrated by

Russell Ayto

ORCHARD BOOKS

For Gabriel and Johnny
U.J.

For Meg the sorceress
R.A.

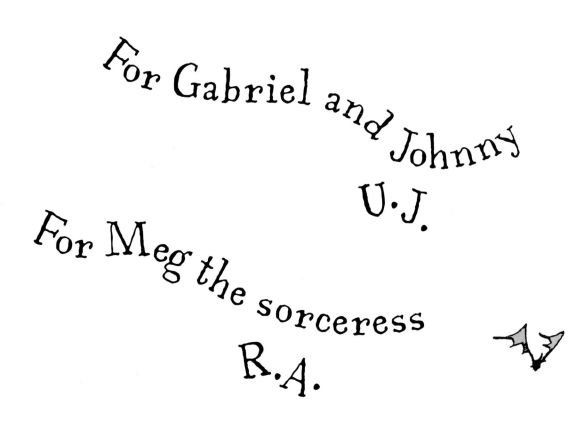

One rainy day, the witch's children went for a walk down the street.

"Look out," said the buses to each other,
"here come the witch's children."
And they hid behind the lorries.

"Look out,"
said the Number
16 Bus, "the witch's children
are coming and that means TROUBLE."

They met Gemma waiting at the bus stop.
"I'm going to the palace," she said, "to see the
Queen's soldiers."
"We'll come too," said the Eldest of the witch's children,
and they all climbed aboard the Number 16 Bus.

The witch's children
bought their tickets
from the bus conductor.
The Little One put
hers in her hat.

"So far no trouble,"
chugged the
Number 16 Bus.

"Oh, no!"

gasped Gemma.
"I've left my money
at home. How will
I pay my fare to
the palace?"

"Like this," said the Eldest
One and he changed Gemma . . .

. . . into . . .

. . . a goose.

"Lay an egg," said the
Eldest One to the goose.

And Gemma the goose laid
a golden egg.

"That will do nicely," said the conductor.

"Thank you," honked Gemma the goose to the Eldest One. "Change me back now, please."

"Can't," said the Eldest One. "I haven't learned how to do that yet."

"Sorry," said the conductor, "geese are not allowed on the bus. Get off, goose."

The goose cried.

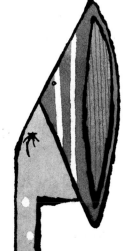

"Now we're in trouble," groaned the Number 16 Bus.
"Now we're in trouble," murmured the passengers.

And the Little One laughed
until she got hiccups.

The goose waddled
off the bus. The tears
dripped down her beak.

"Cheer up, Gemma," said
the Middle One to the goose. "Watch."

And she changed
the bus conductor
into a rich sultan.

And the passengers
into his smiling,
bowing courtiers.

And she changed the
Number 16 Bus into
a magic carpet.

"A goose **is** allowed on a magic carpet," said the Middle One.

"Hold tight,
Miss Goose,"
beamed the sultan,
and they all flew to the palace
on the Number 16 Magic Carpet.

The Queen's soldiers were lined up in her front yard. The magic carpet swished to and fro over their heads. It brushed their busbies off. Nobody could tell whose hat was whose.

"Oi!" shouted the Queen from her balcony. "You on the carpet, you're messing up my army. Come down to land."

"Can't," said the Middle One. "I haven't learned how to do that yet."

"Now we're in trouble,"
puffed the magic carpet.

"Now we're in trouble," wailed the goose,
the sultan and the courtiers.

And the
Little One laughed till she
nearly fell off the magic carpet.
And that cured her hiccups.

The Little One saluted.
"I don't know any spells yet, Your Majesty."
"Well make one up," bellowed the Queen.
So the Little One did.

And all the
Queen's soldiers
changed ...

... into ...

... jam tarts.

"Oo-er!" said the Little One. "Sorry."

The Queen turned purple. She was horribly cross.
"Someone might eat them," she growled.

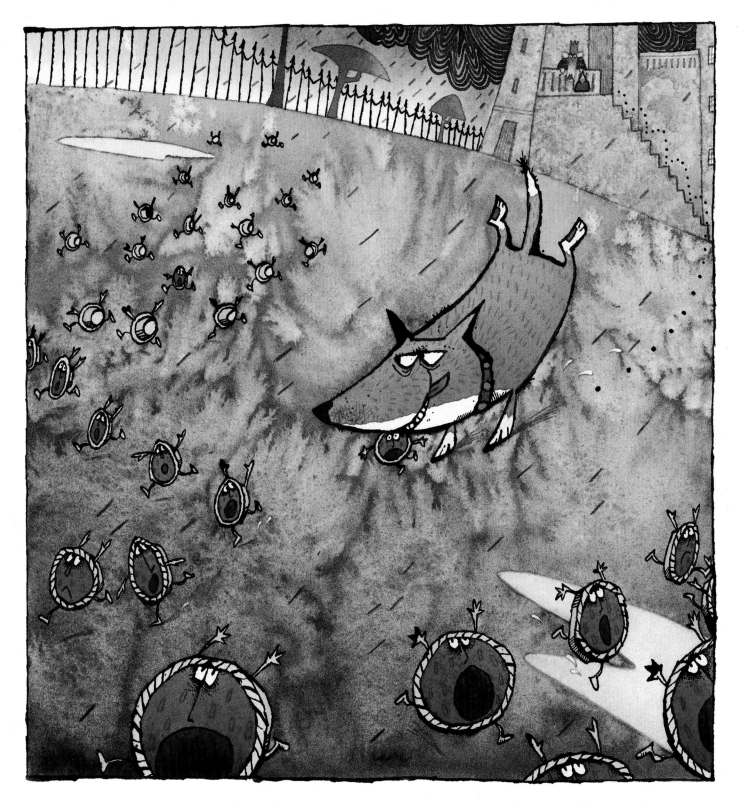

And the Queen's little dog hopped down from the balcony
and picked up a tart in its mouth.

The Duke looked out of the palace window.

"Call for help," shouted the Queen. "The dog's eating the army!"

"Help!" called the Duke.

"Help!" called the goose, the sultan and the courtiers.

"Help!" squeaked the jam tarts.

"We're in a jam, Your Majesty, Ma'am."

The Queen scowled
at the Little One.
"Does your mother know
you're up on a carpet, putting
spells on my soldiers?"

The Little One was scared.
"No," said the Little One,
"but I think I'd like
to fetch her
right now."
"How?" scoffed
the Queen.

"Like this," said the Eldest One, and crossed his eyes.

"Like this," said the Middle One, and showed her knickers.

"Like this," said the
Little One, and chewed up
her bus ticket and spat it out.

"HOW many times..."
said the witch's voice out of the air,
"have I told you children not to do that?"
and then ...

WHOOSH!

. . . there she was
on her broomstick.
"ESPECIALLY,"
the witch continued,
"in front of a Queen."

The witch's children smiled.

"That fetched her," said the Little One.

The witch curtsied to the Queen.

"Mum's here now," said the Little One.

"She'll sort it, Your Majesty."

And the witch did.

She changed the
jam tarts back into soldiers.

She put all the right
busbies back on the
soldiers' heads.

She changed the goose back into Gemma. . .

and the courtiers back
into passengers.

Then she changed
the sultan back into
the bus conductor,

and she changed the magic carpet
back into the Number 16 Bus.

And they were all happy, especially the Little One.

The sun came out and the Queen gave the witch a medal.

Then the witch's children flew away with their mother on her broomstick – over the rainbow and home to play with their pet spiders.